# Dog Watch

BOOK FOUR

## To Catch a Burglar

# Dog Watch

*Keeping the town of Pembrook
safe for people and dogs!*

**BOOK ONE:**
**Trouble in Pembrook**

**BOOK TWO:**
**Dog-Napped!**

**BOOK THREE:**
**Danger at Snow Hill**

**BOOK FOUR:**
**To Catch a Burglar**

# Dog Watch

BOOK FOUR

## To Catch a Burglar

**By Mary Casanova**

**Illustrated by Omar Rayyan**

**Aladdin Paperbacks**
New York  London  Toronto  Sydney

This book is a work of fiction. Any references to historical events,
real people, or real locales are used fictitiously. Other names,
characters, places, and incidents are the product of
the author's imagination, and any resemblance
to actual events or locales or persons,
living or dead, is entirely coincidental.

ALADDIN PAPERBACKS
An imprint of Simon & Schuster
Children's Publishing Division
1230 Avenue of the Americas, New York, NY 10020
Text copyright © 2007 by Mary Casanova
Illustrations copyright © 2007 by Omar Rayyan
All rights reserved, including the right of reproduction
in whole or in part in any form.
ALADDIN PAPERBACKS and colophon are trademarks
of Simon & Schuster, Inc.
Designed by Yaffa Jaskoll
The text of this book was set in Gazette.
Manufactured in the United States of America
First Aladdin Paperbacks edition March 2007
2 4 6 8 10 9 7 5 3 1
Library of Congress Control Number 2006923183
ISBN-13: 978-0-689-86813-9
ISBN-10: 0-689-86813-8

**Dedicated**

to the dogs of Ranier, Minnesota—
past, present, and future

**and**

to Kate, Eric, and Charlie—
and to our family dogs, who have
brought us tears and trouble,
laughter and love
over the years

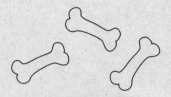

# True:

On the edge of a vast northern Minnesota lake sits a quiet little village where dogs are allowed to roam free. Free, that is, until they get in trouble. One report of a tipped garbage can, nonstop barking, or car chasing, and the village clerk thumbs through doggie mugshots, identifies the dog from its photo, and places a round sticker on the culprit's page. Then she phones the dog's owner. Too many stickers and the troublesome dog is ordered to stay home—tethered to a chain or locked inside the house or yard. No more roaming, and no more adventures with the other dogs of the village.

# Tundra Quits

**In the far** north, winter left grudgingly. By March, seagulls and pelicans returned, waiting for the last snowfall to pass. In April they floated on ice rafts under the trestle bridge, as chunk by chunk, ice melted off the big lake. Villagers waited for spring too. In May the ice was finally gone. The start of the fishing season—or Fishing Opener—was only days away, and the village of Pembrook bustled with activity.

With the other village dogs, Kito and Chester gathered at the fire hydrant outside the post office. They met there every morning—

all sniffs and wags—to catch up on recent news. The dogs had discussed how their owners were forgetting vet appointments, neglecting to walk their dogs, and missing regular feeding times. But this morning's talk was of a more serious nature.

"We were robbed!" Tundra exclaimed. "I'll never be able to hold my head high again."

Kito couldn't believe what he was hearing! Normally Tundra carried her white German shepherd body tall and proud as she circled the other dogs at the fire hydrant. As their leader, she enforced order and discipline, teeth to neck if necessary. But this morning was different.

Tundra's head hung low. She sat heavily on her haunches, waiting for her owner, Mr. Erickson, to pick up his mail. "Find a new alpha dog," she said, eyes cast toward the sidewalk. "I'm useless."

"But there must be an explanation," Kito said, squaring his chow shoulders and stepping closer. "Tundra, nobody gets past *you*!"

"Huh. Well it looks like *somebody has*."

"Criminy biscuits!" Chester exclaimed.

"Tundra, just because you were robbed doesn't mean you throw in the beef bone, hide under the bed, run from the—"

"Chester, stop! I get your point, but it doesn't matter," she said. "What is a dog truly worth if she can't stop a burglar from robbing her own home?"

A sparkling purple truck towing a matching fishing boat roared past, right through a fresh rain puddle, splashing them all. Kito scowled and shook his coat. *Strangers.* A low growl vibrated in his throat. With the Fishing Opener just a few days away, lots of strangers were heading through Pembrook.

Lucky stepped closer, losing her balance temporarily on her three legs. Despite her collision with a car months ago, she had no problem keeping up with the rest of them. "Were you away when the robbery happened?"

Tundra's eyes narrowed. "I have no excuse," she said tartly, sounding for a moment like their usual leader. "I was home."

Kito considered the word: "home." It was in the heart of every dog to love and protect his or her home. And through their efforts in forming Dog Watch, they'd taken that devotion one step further: to keep the whole village safe for people and dogs. If Tundra couldn't stop someone from creeping in and stealing from Mr. Erickson, then something was definitely wrong in Pembrook.

"I'd make a better doormat than a dog," Tundra continued, raising her head for an instant. "Consider this my notice. I'm stepping down as your leader."

"When?" Kito asked, alarmed.

"Now."

This was bad. Kito was stunned into silence.

"Nooooo!" Gunnar protested.

The other dogs joined in, just as Mr. Erickson stepped out of the post office with another villager. "They must have hit my grocery store first," he said to Hank Burton, who constantly chewed his fingernails and had just opened Hank's Treasures, a gift shop across from the grocery store. The dogs listened in.

Mr. Erickson scratched at the white stubble on his face. The burglary must have really upset him, Kito noted. Mr. Erickson was always clean shaven.

"Cleaned out the cash register," he said, "and then climbed the steps to my upstairs home and somehow got past Tundra."

Tundra flinched.

"Didn't take much. Some old stuff. I must have slept through the whole thing." He glanced at Tundra and shook his head. "Guess Tundra did, too. But what doesn't make sense to me is why Tundra didn't wake up."

"Think I should be worried?" Hank asked, biting his fingernails faster. "I mean, I've worked like a dog to get my shop set up."

The dogs exchanged glances. Hank Burton had no idea how hard the dogs of Pembrook worked to keep the village safe!

"What if someone tried to steal from my store? I don't have a big dog to protect it when I go home for the day."

Mr. Erickson glanced at Tundra. "Well, I

have a guard dog. A big one too. Just wasn't enough to stop the burglar."

At that, Tundra dropped her head deeper between her paws and groaned.

"Maybe she's taken ill. Look at her. She's just not herself this morning."

"That's for darn sure."

"Could be that's why the burglar got past her. You think?"

Kito could barely stand to see their leader so defeated. The alpha was at the top, and every dog knew his or her position from the top down. An alpha dog was always in charge, always making decisions. This *new* Tundra made him feel as if his world were topsy-turvy. Their fearless leader couldn't just walk away from her role. The dogs of Pembrook needed her!

"But I doubt anyone would hit twice in a village our size," Mr. Erickson continued.

Hank chomped on his nails. "I hope you're right."

"Well, c'mon, Tundra. Let's go, girl."

Without giving her usual stare-down to

6

the other dogs, Tundra slunk away alongside her owner. Her tail hung low and her body drooped with each step. The Dog Watch team stared, bewildered, as Tundra plodded off with Mr. Erickson and Hank Burton beyond the railroad tracks.

2

the old dog, Indiana, a massive, old
bernaise dog, Indiana. He and the
Mastered, still, wide-eyed. The I too
team waited, breath redust. Broum
sed off with his Dambian and leapt, I
beyond the rescue pack.

# Keeping a Lookout

"**Y'all, this jus'** makes my heart si-ick,"
wailed Muffin, in her Southern drawl. She
stood on her tiny hind legs and rested her
front paws on the fire hydrant. "Tundra is so
mopey," she said, "so low-down in spirit that
I jus' think we mus' do whatever it takes to
cheer her up agin and get her back to her ole
Queen Bee self."

Gunnar shook his head, sending a
length of drool splattering against the fire
hydrant. "Muffin, you are soooo riiiiight."

"The only way we'll get Tundra back to
her old self," Kito said, "is to sniff out the
burglar and catch him!"

"Or her," Lucky added.

"Right. Or her. But somehow we have to make Tundra think she did it."

"Did what?" Chester asked. "Stole from Mr. Erickson? Committed burglary?"

Kito huffed. "No. Caught the burglar."

"Chicken gizzards," Chester said. "How are we gonna do that? If someone got by her in the first place, then we have to be smarter than Tundra and smarter than the burglar. In other words, to use the skills of famed British detective Sherlock Holmes, we must think like the burglar, right?" Chester began pacing, nose to the air, but soon his nose was to the ground. *Snuffle, snuffle, snuff, snuff.* "Whoa! Someone was here last night with pretzels."

"Probablyyyyy someooooone from the tavern." Gunnar, who lived at the tavern, knew that place better than any dog in Pembrook.

"I've got it!" Schmitty said, flapping his black Lab ears back and forth. He turned to Kito. "The burglar must have used some kind of high-tech equipment. I've seen stuff on TV. James Bond, shows like that. Maybe an invisible cloak or night-vision goggles! That's the only way anyone could outsmart Tundra!"

"Schmitty," Kito said, "I believe in Tundra, through and through. But someone snuck past her, and that means we've got a big mystery on our paws. Unfortunately, at this point, we don't know enough. So let's fan out, keep our ears alert for anything unusual, and report back here as we learn more."

The dogs agreed, and then scattered toward all ends of the village.

"Looks like you're the big dog on campus now," Chester said, trotting alongside Kito.

"Temporarily. That's all. I don't want to take Tundra's place—ever! I want her back. We're going to help get her back where she belongs—as Top Dog!"

"Then we've got work to do, don't we, good buddy?"

But Kito didn't answer. His eyes and ears were on the red and white Schwankl Frozen

Foods delivery truck. It rolled past them on Main Street with a driver he'd never seen before. His back hairs bristled. "Everyone is a suspect," he said as they trotted down Pine Street.

"Righto," Chester agreed. "We need to be on full alert!"

Behind the community building, Kito eyed a couple at the tennis courts. Tourists, most likely. Still, they were *strangers*. He veered wide, keeping as much distance as possible between him and them. Unlike most villagers, who wore T-shirts and shorts when they played, this couple was dressed in crisp, white tennis outfits. They smelled new. New clothes, new neon green tennis balls, new racquets, new shoes. And they hit the balls so hard!

*Whack!* The young man hit the ball to the woman.

*Smack!* She slammed it back.

*Crack!* He sent the ball flying up—up—up—and over the fence. Kito kept his eye on it. Down it came in a smooth arc.

Kito stepped right, left, then right again, and it smacked him between the eyes. He yelped, and for a few seconds saw double.

"Finders keepers!" Chester grabbed the ball in his mouth and dashed toward home.

"Hey!" the man yelled. "You little thief! Get back here with that!"

From the corner of his eye, Kito watched the man leap over the tennis net, storm through the court gate, and run down the street—straight toward him! He wasn't going to wait around. He took off after Chester.

They pawed furiously on the front door. "Open up!" Kito barked. Chester whined, the neon green ball gripped firmly in his mouth.

"Coming!" Mrs. Hollinghorst called from inside. When the door opened, the dogs rushed past her and into the attached garage. They darted past Mr. Hollinghorst's legs, scrambled under the workshop table, and hid behind boxes of bolts and screws.

"What's up?" asked Mr. H, peering at them. "Looks like you're hiding."

But Kito and Chester ignored him. Ears perked up, they listened to the conversation at the entry door.

"What seems to be the problem?" came Mrs. H's voice.

"Ma'am, if that beagle lives here, then the problem is that he stole my tennis ball. And I don't buy just any balls. I buy only the best—the 'triple-action-zesty-spin' balls. Now, I admit, sometimes I get a little carried away with my own strength and, well, I hit a ball out of the field, so to speak. You know, over the fence."

"Uh-huh. I see."

"So where is that little thief?"

"Name-calling isn't necessary, Mr. . . . Mr. . . ."

"Mr. Edward."

"Okay, Edward, one moment and—"

"No, not Edward. It's Mr. Ernest Edward."

"Oh, then—whatever your name is—please wait one moment."

Beneath the workbench, Kito said, "I knew your stealing would come back to bite us in the butt. I just didn't think it would happen this soon!"

Chester snuffled the ball. "It's just a little tennis ball. Do you know how many get whacked over the fence? What's one ball?" He nibbled at the green felt coating. "Hmmm, not bad."

Kito narrowed his eyes. "Don't slobber on it."

Mrs. Hollinghorst suddenly reached down and yanked the ball from between Chester's paws. "There it is. And Chester, you look guilty too."

With a chuckle she left, ball in hand.

"Here you go," she said from the front door.

"It's a mucky mess," said Mr. Ernest Edward. "My wife and I thought we'd play a little tennis before the Fishing Opener. We'd have more fun if dogs didn't run free in this village, stealing our tennis balls and causing a general disturbance!"

Under the workbench, Chester whispered, "That wasn't *stealing*. Not really."

"Yeah, well then, what was it?" Kito asked.

"Just a little fun. You know, just for sport."

"I'm sure every thief has their way of looking at it. Seems to me whenever you take something that doesn't belong to you, that's stealing."

"Criminy cripes, Kito. Not when you *find* it."

"Maybe not. But when you *find* it and take off with the owner hollering after your tail, that's a pretty clear case of stealing to me."

Mrs. Hollinghorst's voice sounded strained. "Mr. Edward, did you get what you were looking for?"

"Well, yes. Yes, I did."

"Okay, then. Have a good day."

The door closed firmly, and the dogs eased out of their hiding place.

Mrs. Hollinghorst stepped into the garage. She gazed out the paned windows above the workbench and out toward the bay. "Silly man, that Edward fellow. Now, where was I?" she said cheerily. "Oh, finishing that Wiggling Wiggler lure."

Kito stood on his hind legs, rested his

paws on the edge of the workbench, and surveyed his owners' handiwork. Dozens of hand-carved wooden minnows, ranging from two to eight inches in length, covered the top. The fishing lures were painted in exquisite detail—eyes, fins, and scales—and in every color of the rainbow.

Mr. H held up one wooden lure. With his carving knife, he sliced off peels of golden wood until the shape looked real enough to swim away.

"*Voilá!* This one's ready for your artistry, dear." He handed it to Mrs. H.

Donning the painter's shirt hanging on a nearby hook, she turned to the palette of paints and began brushing bright colors on the pieces of carved wood. Stroke by stroke, dot by dot, scale by scale, she added layers of paint until the fishing lure looked real.

Kito curled in a ball as they worked. He loved the smells of fresh wood and paint and the easy chatter between his owners. Best of all, he felt snug and safe in the garage with them, where he didn't have to worry about strangers stealing from villagers or chasing him down.

He felt downright wonderful, that is, until—

*Knock, knock.*

*Now* who was at the front door? Another *stranger*?

**3**

# To Lure a Burglar

**The knocking on** the entry door continued. Kito's back hairs shot up, and he started barking wildly. All this news of a burglary made him uneasy. He still couldn't believe that anyone could get past Tundra. It made no doggone sense! Scared or not, Kito refused to let a *stranger* and possible burglar get past him. He would stand up—be tough! His heart raced, his feet were in motion, and he barked at the top of his lungs as he bounded for the front door. Chester, on the other hand, dove under the workshop table again and took cover.

"Get a grip, Kito," said Mr. H, and stepped from the garage into the house. With one hand he opened the front door; with the other he grabbed Kito by his collar.

To Kito's relief, standing on the doorstep was their friendly neighbor, Mayor Jorgenson. His balding head glistened with a fresh sprinkling of raindrops. Kito sighed, relieved.

"Come in, Mayor, come in!" said Mr. H, holding the door wide open. "Don't stand out there in the rain!"

"Oh, it's just a May shower. It will pass as quickly as it came. Some poor folks at the tennis courts, though, are none too happy. I just passed them on their way back to Cozy Cabins. Pretty soggy and crabby looking, I'd say."

"Well what brings you over this morning?"

The mayor cleared his throat and stepped inside. "Did ya hear about the burglary at the grocery store?"

The *burglary*. Kito listened closely.

"No, we haven't as much as stepped out to

get our mail yet today. We're knee-deep in our hobby again. Here, come on in. I'll show you," Mr. H said, and led the way to the garage.

"Oh my! What a fine collection! Absolutely stunning!" The mayor picked up one silvery-plum minnow with two silvery barbs attached to its underside. "Some big fish will love this one! With these, you two could win the competition this weekend. You've always made some mighty fine lures."

"Competition?" asked Mr. H.

"Oh, I forget. You two are artist types, with your heads in the clouds half the time." He winked. "Read all about your type when I was working on my doctorate in psychology."

"That so?" said Mrs. H, turning to greet him, her paintbrush poised in midair.

"Yup. You can focus on one thing so well, like your art, Mrs. H, and your, er, writing, Mr. H, but then you don't always see the big picture of what's going on around you, isn't that so?"

Mr. and Mrs. H looked at each other and laughed.

"Why yes, I suppose so," said Mr. H. He picked up another block of wood and began whittling, flake by wooden flake.

"As I was saying, the competition is at the community building this Saturday. After everyone returns from the opening day of fishing, we'll hold the first annual Big Fish, Great Lure contest. A cash prize goes to the biggest fish caught that day—and another prize goes to the best-looking wooden fishing lure."

Mrs. H clasped her hands together. "Honey, sounds like fun. Maybe we should enter."

Mayor Jorgenson picked up the magnifying glass on the table and examined the lures. "I'll be judging, and I'd say you two have some strong contenders here." Then he turned away, his smile slipping, his round face growing serious.

"But back to the burglary. To bring you up to speed, well, it looks like Mr. Erickson's cash register was hit first, with a mere six dollars stolen—in change. Like all smart businesspeople, our grocer deposits his money at the bank at the end of the day. But the burglar didn't know that. Apparently, the burglar then went upstairs, somehow got past Tundra—"

"Past Tundra?" repeated Mrs. H. "That doesn't make sense, does it?"

Mayor Jorgenson shrugged. "Maybe the burglar gave her a sleeping pill."

Chester jumped out from beneath the table. "A sleeping pill!" he said to Kito. "That's it, that's it! And that's why she looked so dopey this morning! It hadn't worn off yet."

"But a burglar," Kito said skeptically, "would have to get *close* to Tundra before he could give her any kind of sleeping pill or shot."

"Criminy. You're right. Nobody could do that."

"Anyway," the mayor went on, "the burglar stole—get this—Mr. Erickson's *entire* wooden lure collection."

Chester sat at the mayor's feet. A wrinkle of concentration formed between his floppy beagle ears.

Mr. H set down the lure he was carving. "You're kidding."

"I wish I were," said the mayor.

This news troubled Kito, and he gave his coat a shake. Poor Mr. Erickson. The grocer was always generous and tossed meat scraps whenever he and Chester stopped at the back of his grocery store.

"Who would go after a fishing lure collection?" asked Mr. H.

"Someone who knows what such lures are worth these days," said the mayor. "Here in Pembrook, where so many of us make and collect these old-style lures, we don't think about the market out there. Some of 'em would garner pretty hefty prices. Hundreds of dollars for some."

"Hundreds?" repeated Mrs. H. "You mean for a whole collection?"

The mayor shook his head. "Nope. Sometimes for just *one* lure. The old lures—the antiques. That's what this might be about. That's why I wanted to let you know about the burglary. If someone stole Mr. Erickson's collection, they might keep snooping around for more. I thought I'd better warn you."

Mrs. H laughed, holding up two lures. "Well, we're just copying our designs from an old book." She pointed to the book on the worktable, dusted with wood shavings. "I don't think we need to worry about anyone wanting these."

Mr. Jorgenson swiped his hand across the top of his glossy head. "Oh, don't be too quick to say that. From what I see," he said, stretching his hand toward their table, "you have a Silver Flash, a Dinger, a Shur Strike, a Moonlight Dreadnaught, and a Shakespeare. If you can fool me that those are old and valuable, then I swear you can fool anyone." He chuckled. "I should know."

Kito shot Chester a look, then pointed his nose toward the workshop table. "Wooden fishing lures," he said. "Just the bait we need to catch the burglar—with Tundra's help, of course!"

"Good gravy train!" Chester started to wag his tail. "You're brilliant, Kito!" He wagged it so hard that he knocked a small can of paint off a step stool. The can spilled a puddle of paint over his paws and then Kito's, too. The dogs jumped away, leaving green prints across the cement floor.

"Oh, no!" said Mrs. H. "You're making a fine mess! I shouldn't have left that can there."

Kito glanced back at the can: "Emerald Green." He'd like to tell Chester what exact shade of paint they were wearing, but he liked to keep his ability to read a secret.

"That's it. Outside with you two," said Mr. H, pushing the button for the garage door. The door rose slowly, and the dogs scooted under it and out into the rain. They sped down Pine Street to the fire hydrant, leaving smudged and watery green prints in their wake.

# Green Means Go

**"Green means go,"** Chester called. "Race you to the fire hydrant!"

As they zipped around the corner of the community building, they smacked right into Mr. Cutler. Rain dripped from his rain hat and jacket—and his mustache, as well— but he didn't seem to mind being outside. He squared his hands to his hips and scolded them. "Hey, boys, what's your hurry? You nearly took my legs out!"

The dogs sat back, hard. Kito wagged his tail across the wet grass. Chester inched forward on his belly, then licked Mr. Cutler's outstretched hand.

"Oh, it's okay. Just startled me, that's all. I'm not really angry at you two. How could I be? You're my favorite dogs in all of Pembrook." Then he looked at their paws and laughed. "Looks like you two got in some trouble again, huh? Oh, well, we all make mistakes sometime. You still get treats." He reached into his overalls pocket and produced two biscuits. "Here you go."

The dogs took them gently, careful not to scrape Mr. Cutler's fingers with their teeth. They'd learned that if they weren't polite, they wouldn't get biscuits at all. That's the way it was with Mr. and Mrs. H.

Then they set off again toward the hydrant.

Across from the post office and outside the tavern door, Gunnar sat in the rain, working himself up into a song. With his eyes closed, he tilted back his head, stretched out his neck of skin folds, and pointed his nose toward the sodden sky.

"I'm soooooo blue," he sang. "Without

yooooou! Tell meeee truuuuue! What'll I doooooo?"

Kito and Chester trotted to his side and sat, waiting for Gunnar to finish. But then he started up again, "I'm sooooo blue . . . without yoooooouu . . ."

Kito butted in. "Gunnar."

The basset hound opened his eyes. "Oooooh. I didn't think anyoooone was listening."

"You miss Tundra that bad?" Chester whispered. "You poor guy."

"Well, noooo. Just singing aaaaa juuuuuke-box song." With his blood-shot, droopy eyes, he looked at Chester's and Kito's feet. "Greeeeen?"

"Paint spill," Chester said. "Hey, Kito has figured out how we're going to catch that burglar and get Tundra back to her rightful position again."

"Yoooou doooon't say. With paaaaint?"

"Not exactly," said Kito. "But I have an idea. Want to send out an alert with that baritone voice of yours and call in a meeting?"

Gunnar drew a breath, expanded his deep basset-hound chest, and called out in a howl, "Dog Watch uniiiiiiiite!"

His voice echoed off the bay, off the village buildings along Main Street, and off the post office itself. Then Gunnar joined Chester and Kito outside the post office. Within minutes, dogs of all sizes and from every corner of the village gathered at the hydrant.

Despite plump raindrops, Schmitty was all smiles and wags, jumping up and down. "Great! I'm excited! I'm ready! What's the plan?"

"Here's the skinny," Chester started. "With Kito's brilliant brain always keeping us safe, we have a plan. Right, Kito?"

Kito cleared his throat. "Well, uh . . ." He wished Tundra would just return. He hated having to step in and take charge. He'd rather work behind the scenes and gather information, he'd rather discuss "action plans" with their alpha dog, hold "dog summits," as he thought of them, but he really did *not* like being the spokesdog. "Well," he began again, looking at the dozen dogs that had gathered. Even the two neighboring Tweet pups, Snowball and Chocolate, who had grown long and lanky, had made it to the emergency meeting.

"It's not much, but we have a lead," Kito announced.

"Y'all fixin' to tell us it's green paint?" Muffin asked, breaking into giggles. She started grooming her wet, white legs. "Puddles are bad 'nough. You ain't gonna get me walkin' through paint, no matter what y'all say."

"Muffin, you little sugarplum," Chester said, "just hear him out."

"It's simple," Kito said. "Wooden fishing lures."

Lucky arched her back, stretching. "I don't get it."

"That's what the burgar stole from Mr. Erickson," Kito explained. "So now that we

31

know what the burglar wants, we can bait him and catch him." He started to pace, back and forth. "We need to put out a lure where our criminal will see it."

Schmitty wagged his tail. "I know, I know! Right on the post office steps! Everyone goes in and out. We can watch and wait. The one who picks it up will be our guy."

"Or gal," Lucky said. "We don't yet know."

"Beefy biscuits!" Chester exclaimed. "Not the post office steps! Anyone will pick up a lure, just so the next person doesn't step on it. Ever had a lure in your paw? Well, I have, and it's not a pretty sight. Someone left one on the beach last year, and I ended up going to the vet to have it taken out. Leaving it on the post office steps is definitely out. Whose idea was that, anyway?" He looked at Schmitty.

"Well, what's *your* idea, you big-mouth beagle?" Schmitty's back hairs ruffled in warning. Chester's tail went up like a flagpole. They growled and stared each other down.

"Remember, I'm the only dog in Pembrook

with genuine, certified AKC papers," Chester said.

"Oh, yeah? Well, I was born and bred right here in Pembrook. That counts for something in my book. Besides, how do we know you're not making up the American Kennel Club bit? Have you ever produced your papers to show us? Have you?"

Chester and Schmitty went nose to nose.

"I could prove it if I was tall enough to get my papers off the fridge. You'd see. So a little respect is not too much to ask—"

"Enough, you two!" Kito stepped between them. "Do I have to act like a police dog too? It's enough that our leader has stepped down. The burglar, remember? Anyone else have an idea where to plant the bait?"

"On one of the docks," Chocolate piped up. For a puppy, he was a pretty quick thinker. "That's where people often fish."

"Good suggestion, Chocolate," Kito said, "but couldn't anyone pick it up and use it for fishing? Might think it fell from someone's tackle box."

"Jolly right," Chester said, pressing himself back into the middle of things again. "And we don't know that our burglar even likes fishing. The wooden lures, especially the old ones, are worth money."

"I knooooow," Gunnar said. "The tavern. Lots of tooourists go there."

"That's it!" Kito said. "Now we're getting somewhere. Since you live there, Gunnar, you could place the bait where everyone will see it. What do you say?"

"Suuure. If I stretch waaaaay up, I could get it on the couuuunter."

Willow, the smallest golden retriever in the village, trotted up to the others. "Sorry I'm late," she said, shaking her coat. "I kept whining at the back door, but my owner wasn't getting the message!" She cocked her golden head. Even with rain-soaked ears and face, she was the prettiest dog in the whole village.

Chester nudged Kito in the shoulder and whispered, "Hey, don't go dreamy on us, lover dog."

Kito cleared his throat. "Yes, yes. Well

then, now where were we? First, Willow, I'd better bring you up to speed." He told her about their plan to plant the bait, then said, "And now we need a wooden fishing lure. A valuable one. Anyone have any ideas?"

The dogs all chimed up at once.

"My owner has lots!"

"At home in our garage."

"Sure do! Plenty!"

Kito shook and rainwater flew from his coat in silvery beads. "Wait, if we have to take the bait from home, then that's stealing too. That won't work."

"Sometimes," Chester said, "you have to think like a criminal to catch a criminal, remember?"

"Yeah, but stealing is stealing."

"Not really," Willow said. "Woody, my owner, he's a great fishing guide. He has zillions of lures. If I borrow one, I promise you that I'll return it to Woody—just as soon as we catch the burglar. So that's not really stealing, is it?"

"Well, I think it is," Kito said.

"Buddy, you take things way too seriously," Chester told him.

Kito looked from dog to dog. "I appreciate your willingness to volunteer, but if I'm asking you to do something that might get you in trouble, then I think I'd better do it myself. Mr. and Mrs. H have a good collection of lures. Chester and I will find a way to sneak one out and get it to Gunnar to plant at the tavern. I still don't like it, but this is our only good plan so far."

"Oh, Kito," Willow said, stretching her back. Her lashes were long and black, and Kito couldn't help staring at her. "You're so, so—noble."

"I have another word for it," Chester said, stepping closer to Willow's side.

"What's that?" Willow asked demurely.

"Rock-headed."

At that moment lightning zigzagged through the overhead clouds—a shaft of white light against darkening sky—and the dogs froze. In less than a second, a boom followed that shook Kito to his paws. He didn't need to give an order to leave. Every dog knew that thunder and lightning were reason enough!

The dogs scattered, each to the safety of his or her own home, except for Gunnar, who barked outside the tavern until the door opened.

When the Hollinghorsts opened their front door, Chester beelined inside and hid under their upstairs bed. Kito squeezed into the corner behind the piano, and with each *crack* and *boom*, he trembled like a scared puppy.

**5**

# Going After Trouble

**Curled into a** ball, Kito cowered behind the shelter of the piano. He hated to admit to himself that storms made him jumpy, but they did. Even if he wasn't registered like Chester, his ancestors once guarded the royal palaces in China. He was a disgrace to his chow breeding.

Eyes closed tight with each boom of thunder, he had way too much time to think. Too much time on his paws. He pictured himself creeping into the garage and *stealing* one of his owners' carefully hand-painted fishing lures. He shuddered at the thought. His very own owners. Inexcusable! How could he do such a thing? He'd be going against his own sense of right and wrong. But try as he might, he couldn't think of another way to catch the burglar. Dog Watch needed to set a trap. Put out the bait. Lure in the nasty, no-good thief. That's all there was to it.

By late in the afternoon the storm clouds quieted, and Chester and Kito came out of their hiding places. They met nose to nose in the living room.

"Been napping?" Chester asked. They never liked to admit to each other how much they were afraid of storms. Some things were better left unsaid.

"Yeah, sort of," Kito said. "Thinking mostly. And you?"

"Yup, just thinking. You know, resting."

*Ding-dong!* The doorbell rang. *Ding-dong!*

Finally! Something they could do—bark! They both started woof-woofing at full pitch. A shadowy figure stood on the other side of the etched glass door. Kito didn't recognize the silhouette of a man with narrow shoulders and long legs. And his ears picked up a melody of some sort. The man was humming.

Mr. and Mrs. H stepped from the attached garage to the door. "Yes?" Mrs. H said, opening the door wide.

Kito growled and Chester's back hairs flagged.

"Boys, it's okay," Mr. H said. "Time to order a few food favorites."

Kito glanced out and saw the Schwankl Frozen Foods delivery truck parked outside. The rain had left the truck's red and white paint glistening clean.

"Hi, folks, I'm Jeremy Jones," the man said, shaking hands with the Hollinghorsts. "While Betty's on vacation for the next week, I'm filling in."

"Oh, that's right," said Mrs. H, with a wistful expression. "She'd been talking about that dream for years. *Hawaii.* Good for her! I hope she's having the time of her life."

"You folks need anything this week?" He handed them a Schwankl Frozen Foods flyer.

"I don't think I can live without jalapeno poppers," said Mr. H. "Better get a bag of those."

Mrs. H tapped the flyer with her forefinger. "Strawberry-rhubarb pie is on sale? Better get two of those."

"Better add frozen vanilla yogurt to put on your pie," Mr. H added with a wink.

Kito glanced at Chester and then at the open garage door beyond. He had hoped to wait until the Hollinghorsts were asleep, but he suddenly realized that that wouldn't work. He couldn't turn a handle. He wouldn't be able to get into the garage on his own at night. This might be their only chance to get in, grab the lure, and get out again. "C'mon," he said, "follow me."

They veered through the open door to the garage. Across the workshop table, fishing lures beckoned like Liver Snaps. Kito stood on the chair beside the table and quickly surveyed dozens of lures. So many sizes! So many different-colored lures! How would he know which lure would interest their burglar?

Then he spotted the book about lures. It was left open to a page about "collector" lures that Mrs. H had tried to copy with her paintbrush. He read to himself:

> *The Trouble-Jig dates back to l897. This delightful lure, with its green and gold layering and carefully painted silver speckles, is a favorite among collectors. Today's market brings anywhere from $350 to $700, depending on the lure's condition.*

Amazing! That was exactly the kind of bait he needed. A valuable lure!

"What if you get your mouth on those barbs?" Chester asked. "This is making me squeamish. Don't stick yourself or you'll end up at the vet. A lure in the paw, that's one thing, but—jumping jack terriers—you don't want to get a barb stuck in your muzzle!"

"Well, that's not my intention," Kito said. "But thanks for the advice." He scanned the table. His owners had certainly been busy. He kept looking back and forth from the book to the lures, trying to find a Trouble-Jig.

"Hurry," Chester said. "That Jeremy Jones guy just left to get the frozen foods from his truck. It will only take a minute or two, then the Hollinghorsts will be back. Don't lose your chance. Dog Watch is counting on you!"

There. Finally he saw it. The green and gold lure with speckled silver dots. That Mrs. H was quite an artist. It matched the photo in the book perfectly! He stretched across, careful not to disturb several freshly painted lures, and gently picked up the Trouble-Jig in his teeth. With an extremely soft bite, he held the lure, lips stretched wide. "This isn't easy," he said.

"Okay," Chester said, "you need to get out of the garage, sneak past the Hollinghorsts, and hide the lure outside. That way you can pick it up later and get it to Gunnar at the tavern."

"Right," Kito said, the lure's barbs dangling from the edges of his mouth. "How am I going to do that?"

"I'll create a distraction. They'll let me out first, then you come right on my heels. Just keep those barbs away from my butt."

"Okay. Go!"

Chester let loose with an earsplitting "Woo-woo-wooooooo! Woo-woo-wooooooo!" He raced into the house, in and out of their owners' legs, then toward the lakeside sliding doors.

"What in the world is his problem?" Mr. H said.

Chester pawed at the glass, crying louder and louder. "Woo-woo-wooooo!"

"Chester, that's enough," said Mr. H, but Chester built up his volume and pitch to an unbelievably irritating crescendo.

"Here are your items!" Jeremy Jones called from the entry door. He strained his voice above Chester's racket. "Your total is—"

"Just a minute. I have to let my dog out. He's worked up over a chipmunk or some nonsense. He's making so much noise, I can't even think!" Mr. H slid open the glass door and Chester flew out, his beagle ears catching the wind like two sails.

Kito raced out behind him, the wooden Trouble-Jig dangling carefully from his mouth. He hoped his owners didn't see him.

"Phew! Enough of that," said Mr. H, as he closed the sliding door behind the two dogs.

Chester kept baying, nose to the ground, snuffling fiercely from the rock garden to the dock. "There really were chipmunks here!" he cried. "Woo-woo-woooooo!"

Kito headed for the woodpile. He found the perfect spot to hide the lure: a dank, musty opening between two aging logs. He dropped it in and sat back on his haunches and looked around. Mr. and Mrs. H were still inside. Mission successful, so far.

But a wave of shame spread from his muzzle to the tip of his curved tail. He had *stolen*. His head drooped down. He had gone against his owners. He could only hope that his action would come to some good. If not, he was no better than the burglar that Dog Watch was after.

And yet, he had done it for his buddies, his comrades, Mr. Erickson, the mayor, and his owners. Kito sniffed a breath of fresh air. He had done his dog-sworn duty for Dog Watch!

He had done something brave, hadn't he?

# Lost Opportunity

**"Well, what's shakin'?"** Chester asked, wagging his whole body as he approached the woodpile. "Did you hide it?"

"I did."

"Good dog!" Chester said teasingly. "And you're so *noble*!"

"Oh, knock it off."

"Not up for a little joking? You should be feeling good!"

"I feel terrible. I still don't know about this plan. Maybe I should put the lure back in the garage right away."

"Kito, are you kidding me? You're doing

no such thing. We need to catch that burglar. And if we don't have the right bait, we'll never catch that louse!"

"Well, that's true. I'll feel better when we get the real thief and get Tundra back in charge."

"For now," Chester said, "just act normal. We'll have to wait for the cover of darkness to deliver the lure to the tavern. From there, Gunnar will plant the bait."

Together they trotted along the boundaries of their yard, sniffing and marking, making sure to follow their normal routine. They found nothing unusual, and that was good. They rounded the corner of the house as the Schwankl Frozen Foods truck pulled away and down the street.

That evening, when the Hollinghorsts went canoeing, Chester and Kito made themselves scarce. Usually they liked to go along (even though they once tipped the canoe when an otter swam past). But this evening they stayed clear of the dock.

"See you two shortly," said Mrs. H, waving

from beneath her wide-brimmed straw hat. The sun sank, spreading red jam across the horizon.

As soon as the canoe rounded the bend, Kito snatched the lure from the woodpile, and he and Chester took off.

They met Gunnar behind the tavern as scheduled. "I'm ready toooo dooooo my part for the teeeeeeam."

Kito set the lure carefully on the ground. "See that you get it back to me in the same condition. No teeth marks. Not a dent. My owners spent lots of time making this Trouble-Jig."

"Is that what yooooou call it?"

"Yup. And if anyone—anyone at all—starts looking at it and seems extra interested in the lure, they're probably the one we're after. So no sleeping. Stay awake until closing. Can you do that, Gunnar?"

"Ooooooh, sure. I'll meet you in the moooorning."

Chester chimed in, "And easy on the drool. Try to return it dry."

Gunnar didn't answer. He humphed, picked up the lure in his big mouth, and lumbered through the tavern's open back door. Country music floated out over parked pickup trucks.

"Hey," Kito said. "Hear that?"

"What?" Chester replied, ears twitching.

"That's the same music Jeremy Jones was humming."

Chester scrunched his forehead and listened. "All I hear is that someone's heart got broke or something."

"You don't get it. Jeremy Jones. You know, the Schwankl delivery guy? But then, I don't know, maybe his humming a country tune doesn't mean much of anything, does it?"

"Lots of people hum country tunes, Kito. You're getting a little uptight. Maybe you should try to relax a little. You know, take a break, put your legs up, lay low . . ."

Just then, something caught Kito's attention. Among the trucks and cars outside the tavern, Kito noticed the same sparkling purple pickup that had splashed them earlier outside the post office. His back hairs bristled. "That truck," he whispered, pointing his nose toward the vehicle. "I don't have a good feeling about it."

"Good buddy," Chester said, pointing his black nose homeward, "unless you quit worrying so much, you're never going to live up to Sherlock Holmes detective standards. You need a rest."

"Maybe you're right. We'll head home, get some shut-eye, and see what tomorrow brings. It's been a doggone long day."

# Deepening Shadows

**As Kito and Chester** ambled toward home, shadows gathered deep and dark around them. Kito knew he should feel encouraged. By tomorrow morning, Gunnar would know the burglar's identity. But in his gut he felt a braided knot of worry, guilt, and hope. He still felt terrible about stealing. That would never be okay. But now he felt a thread of hope, too.

"Hey, Kito," Chester said as they trotted down Pine Street side by side.

"Yeah?"

"Remember Dumbeat?" Chester said.

"I remember. That dog's been gone a couple of years."

"I miss him sometimes, that's all."

"Yeah, but he was always nipping at kids and stealing their shoes from the beach. That's why he was finally *banished*. His owners were told he could never come back. What made you think of him?"

"Barkin' beef bites! I don't know. Maybe it's being out late at night. Dumbeat used to roam the streets at night, knew every nook and corner of Pembrook. He might have been a help at a time like this. Can't picture him in New York City with his owners. Poor dog. What kind of life is it to always be on a leash or in a fenced yard?"

"If Mr. and Mrs. H find that I stole from them, maybe they'll *banish* me, too!"

"Never thought of that possibility. Guess we better get this case wrapped up, and fast."

Just as they approached home, Kito noticed something across the street at the Tweets' house. Slinking alongside the house,

a flash of dark motion slid through the shadows and disappeared.

Chester's head swung in the same direction, his nose twitching. They stopped.

Watching.

Sniffing.

"That was too big to be Sheeba!" Kito whispered. Ever since the Tweets adopted Chocolate and Snowball, the terrorizing cat had been making herself scarce. Kito absorbed everything, straining for a clue. A breeze carried rich scents of buds opening and sun-warmed earth, and the sound of spring peepers with a high-pitched chorus from a distant pond.

"I know I saw something," he said.

"I'll get a beat on the smell," Chester said, nose to the ground. *Snuffle, snuffle, snuff, snuff.*

At that moment the entry light flashed behind them from their house. Kito glanced back. Mr. H stepped outside in his pajamas. "Where've you two boys been? Thought you'd be waiting on the dock for us. You've had us worried. Time for bed. Come in now."

Chester and Kito didn't budge.

"If we obey," Kito whispered, "we can't go check things out at the Tweets'—whatever or whoever that was!"

"Chester, Kito—come!" This time Mr. H's command was firm.

Kito felt all his spirit of adventure drain away. He didn't want to go against his owners. They were the ones who supplied him with good food, daily scratchings, and a place to call home. He'd already stolen from them today. He had no choice now but to obey.

He and Chester started slowly toward Mr. H, who shook his head at them. "You two sure are acting strange. Must be something out there that's got your interest." He held the door wide open. But as they crossed the landing, car lights cut along Pine Street toward them. Kito and Chester spun back around. It was the Tweet family. They parked their pickup across the street, and out spilled the redheaded family, with Chocolate and Snow-ball. The puppies started sniffing, barking, and running in circles around their yard.

Kito's back bristled. "They found some-thing!"

"Chicken chicklets! Let's go find out!"

"Boys—just mind your own business!" said Mr. H. "There's no need—"

But Chocolate's barking had changed everything. "Someone's been here while we were gone!"

Snowball joined in. "Dog Watch! Chester! Kito!"

At that, Kito and Chester bolted away from Mr. H and sped across the driveway to the Tweets'. The whole family stared at the open door to their church-house. Not a single light was on inside.

"I'm sure we closed the door. Somebody broke in!" cried Mrs. Tweet, running her hands through her thick red hair. "Who would do such a thing?"

"What if someone's still in there?" wailed Emmaline, grabbing her dad's hand.

Zoey squealed, "Maybe it's the same person who stole from the grocery store and Mr. Erickson!"

"Oh, boy," said Mr. Tweet. "I'm not feeling very good about this."

Kito and Chester ran after the puppies, who raced and darted in a panic around their yard. "Here we had our first big chance to be watchdogs," Chocolate said, "and we were stuck riding to and from Zoey's piano recital!"

"We could have stopped them!" Snowball cried. "I know we could have!"

By this time the mayor, the mayor's mother, and the Hollinghorsts had come over to see what was going on. They clustered closer to the Tweets, as if there was safety in numbers. This was usually true for dogs. Maybe it was true for humans, too. Finally, Mr. and Mrs. Tweet stepped inside their house and filled it with bright light. Seconds later they stepped out again.

Kito and Chester hovered at their owners' legs.

"The only thing missing," Mrs. Tweet explained, "is our collection of wooden fishing lures."

"Did you make them?" asked Mayor Jorgenson's mother. "I've been working on a few of my own down in the basement."

Mrs. Tweet frowned. "It was our spring Girl Scout project. The girls were going to enter them in the competition this weekend."

Zoey started to cry. "Mine was going to win!"

"No," Emmaline cried, "mine was!"

Mayor Jorgensen stepped forward. "Two thefts in Pembrook are two too many! We need to get to the bottom of this!"

Before long, Kito and Chester trailed the Hollinghorsts back home. First thing, their owners stepped into the garage and flipped on the light.

"Looks like our collection is secure," said Mrs. H, with a grateful nod.

Mr. H walked closer. "Wait. Something's not quite right. I can't put my finger on it."

He scanned their hand-painted lures. "Why, there seems to be one missing."

"Honey, that's so odd. Who would steal just one?"

Kito's tail drooped low. He willed it to curl up over his back. He didn't need to look guilty, even if he felt it.

"Well, that's the weirdest thing in the world," said Mr. H. "My Trouble-Jig is missing." He stooped to his knees and looked under the table. "The one Grandpa Pete gave to me." He stood up and shook his head.

Mrs. H patted his shoulder. "Oh honey, that's terrible."

Mr. H's chin trembled. "We used to fish Rainy Lake together. Caught my first northern pike on that lure." He put his face in his hands. "I didn't plan on putting it in the competition. I didn't care about all that. It means more to me than a ribbon or money ever could!"

"Don't worry, dear. It'll show up, you just wait and see. I'm sure we misplaced it somewhere."

Mr. H drew a deep breath, then let it out again. "I suppose so. I hope you're right. Someone would have stolen the whole collection if they were looking for lures, don't you think?"

"That's what I think. Still, there are some strange goings-on in Pembrook."

"At least we have our dogs," Mr. H said, his arm around his wife's waist, and looked down at the dogs. "You'll keep a lookout for us, won't you, boys? You won't let anyone break in, will you?"

Kito and Chester wagged their tails.

"I hope we can protect our home," Kito whispered, as they followed the Hollinghorsts upstairs to bed.

Chester met his glance. "Me too, good buddy. Me too."

# 8

# Doggedly Determined

**Morning sunlight skittered** across the bay and tickled Kito's eyes. He stretched and left his dog bed to wake Chester, who was only three, but snoring like a white-muzzled old dog. *Uh-heeee-hoooooo! Uh-heeee-hooooo!*

"Hey, get up," Kito said, nose to the edge of the Hollinghorsts' bed.

*Uh-heeee-hooooo!*

"Psst! Chester."

Chester's head shot upright. He sniffed the air. "What? What's wrong?"

"Are you still dreaming?" Kito snapped. "What do you mean, what's *wrong*? The

Tweets were robbed just last night! *Plus* we need to see what Gunnar found out at the tavern. *And* I need to return the Trouble-Jig. The sooner the better. How was I to know that lure was so valuable to Mr. H?"

"Diggity-do, Kito. I was in a good sleep." He arched his back and yawned. "And I was dreaming of a little cocker spaniel who couldn't take her eyes off me, and—"

"I thought it was Willow you were sweet on."

"Ha! Me? You mean, you!"

Kito strutted away. "C'mon, we don't have time to argue."

Downstairs, Mrs. H was wrapped up in a quilt on the couch, reading the newspaper. Mr. H was busy working on a crossword puzzle on the crate they used as a coffee table. Coffee steamed in their mugs.

"Stick to our routines," Kito said. "Can't let them suspect anything unusual."

The dogs leaned into their owners' legs to get a good morning scratching. Then they whined and stared at their empty dog dishes until they were filled with Hearty Hound, which they finished in record time. After that, they headed outside.

Robins hopped about the yard, stopping to pull worms from the dewy ground. The dogs let the birds alone but scouted the yard for other sorts of intruders.

"A chipmunk passed through last night," Chester declared, "but that's it."

"Coast is clear," Kito said.

As the sun climbed in the east, they tore side by side down Pine Street to find Gunnar. At the post office, the flag wasn't flying yet from the flagpole. The sign on the post office door read CLOSED. Not a single dog was to be seen.

"There he is," Chester said, pointing his snout toward Gunnar across the street outside the tavern. Curled in a big white and brown ball, Gunnar snored. *Rup, rup, rup, whoooooooooo! Rup, rup, rup, whoooooooooo!*

Kito and Chester trotted over.

"Top of the morning to you!" Chester chimed.

Gunnar grunted and snorted but didn't move a muscle.

"Sorry to wake you so early," added Kito. "But the Tweets were robbed last night. I'm hoping the burglar swung by the tavern before it closed. Any luck?"

Gunnar breathed heavily, settling back to sleep again.

*Rup, rup, rup, whoooooooooo!*

"Criminy! I don't snore like that, do I?"

"Yup. Just in a higher pitch."

Chester sniffed Gunnar's face and ears. "Funny, but he smells like, like—I can't quite put my nose on it. Pizza. Definitely pizza."

"Sheeeesh!" Gunnar complained, rousting himself awake and standing slowly. "A dog can't eeeeven sleeeeeep around heeere."

"Not when there's a mystery to solve," Kito said. "Well? Did you plant the wooden lure on the counter?"

"Just give me a description, red eyes," Chester said, "and I'll hunt him down, bring him to justice, see that he's locked up forever where the sun don't shine, see that he serves—"

"Nooooope. Noooo luck."

Kito stood squarely. He didn't want to push, but Gunnar had to know more. "Wait, didn't anyone show interest in the lure? Certainly someone must have looked at it, maybe picked it up and wondered about it, said something—"

"Noooope."

"Then, well, darn it. Guess I'd better return it to my owners—on the double, too. Mr. H has fond memories of that lure. I mean, that thing's a real antique!"

"Well, I can't quite doooooo that."

"What do you mean, you can't?" Kito asked.

"I mean, a few peeeeople loooooked at it. I kept watching. Then out of noooooowhere, I found a sliiiiiice of piiiiiiiza on the flooooooor."

"Yeah?" Chester asked. "What kind?"

"Doesn't matter what kind," said Kito, growing impatient. "Just tell me where the Trouble-Jig is and I'll get it. I need to return it."

"That's what I'm tryyyyying toooo tell yoooooou. Someone stooole it!"

"Stole it?" Kito could barely get the words out. The morning sun slowly warmed the ground, but Kito's paws turned icy with dread. "And you didn't see who it was?"

"Noooope. When I finished myyyyyyy piiiiiiza, I looooked and the luuuuure was . . ." With a heavy groan, Gunnar flopped down.

"Poppin' pupcorn!" Chester said under his breath. "This is *not* good."

Kito remembered the time he ate too much ice cream. He felt that way now. Sick to his stomach. It would have been bad enough to lose any one of his beloved owners' carefully carved and painted lures. How was he to know that he'd picked their most valuable lure, the Trouble-Jig that Mr. H had used as a boy and inherited from his grandfather? If he was human, he'd smack himself in the forehead with the back of his hand. Instead he gave his coat a frustrated, furious shake.

"It's all my fault," he said with a moan. "I should have known that stealing could lead to no good. Now I've torn something valuable from the very heart of Mr. H." He felt weak and dizzy. His legs wobbled like an unsteady newborn pup's. He closed his eyes.

Chester nudged him with his wet nose. "Kito! Get a grip! Pull it together, pal. You can't lose it at a time like this!"

"I don't want to be in charge anymore. I'm making a mess of things!"

Chester and Gunnar waited in silence.

Finally Kito opened one eye, then the other.

"Well," Chester asked, "are you done with your pity party?"

Kito humphed. He wished he could be like other dogs and just stretch out and forget his cares. But that simply wasn't in him. He couldn't look the other way when trouble was on the village's every doorstep. At last he filled his chest with air, then let it out again.

"Someone's got us on the run," he said. "We're so turned around we don't know our tails from our noses. But that doesn't mean we give up."

"Nooooo waaaaaay." Gunnar shook his head, and Chester jumped clear of the stringy drool cast in his direction.

"No, we're not going to give up, but we need help," Kito continued. "We need Tundra, that's what. She has to come back to the pack and fulfill her rightful duty as alpha dog of Pembrook. She'll know what to do."

Kito started off toward Erickson's Very Fine Grocery Store beyond the railroad tracks. Chester and Gunnar flanked him, struggling to keep up.

"Aren't yoooou scaaared she'll snap at yooooou?" Gunnar wheezed.

Kito trotted on, doggedly determined.

"It's a risk I have to take."

9

# Eerie News

**The grocery store** was busy with villagers coming and going. Kito, Chester, and Gunnar parked themselves at the base of the steps, waiting for Tundra to show up.

Mr. Erickson stepped out, wiping his hands on his white grocer's apron. "Bet you boys are looking for Tundra," he said.

So many times, when Mr. Erickson spoke with them, Kito could swear that the man truly read dogs' minds. He remembered the definition of "empathy," a word he'd looked up in the dictionary: "Understanding so intimate that the feelings, thoughts, and motives of one are readily understood by another." By that definition, *empathy* was like a silent language—the language between some people and dogs. Mr. Erickson certainly had a lot of *empathy* for dogs.

Once again clean shaven, Mr. Erickson tilted his head. "I wish Tundra would go outside too. She's just lying around upstairs. Something's not right with her. It's like she's depressed or something."

Mr. Erickson, Kito figured, would score superhigh in *empathy*.

The dogs sat, their noses pointed right toward Mr. Erickson, their ears catching every word. "Oh, but I'm rambling, aren't I?" he said. "You dogs don't care about an old man's prattle. You're looking for *treats*."

Kito wagged his tail, wanting to show Mr. Erickson he really *did* understand every word he'd said.

Mr. Erickson smiled. "*Treats*. Now that's one word you dogs understand. Meet me around back." Then he stepped inside the store, and the dogs started for the back of the building.

Kito took two steps but stopped short beside the newspaper holder. He couldn't take his eyes off the headline. "Go ahead," he said to Chester and Gunnar. "I'll catch up with you." As soon as they rounded the corner, he read the front-page story:

VILLAGERS GRIPPED IN FEAR
*Pembrook residents have reason to keep their doors locked. "Three burglaries in three days is alarming," reported Mayor Jorgenson. "First the grocery store was robbed, then the Tweets' residence, and Pembrook's newest resident, Angelica Phillips, reported a burglary at her home late last night."*

"That's Bear's owner!" Kito said under his breath. Bear, the village's only Newfoundland dog, was nearly as big as a yearling bear. What person in their right mind would try to get past him? He shuddered. Events were turning downright eerie. Bulky dogs like Bear and Tundra should be scary enough to keep any intruder away. What was going on? Shivers zipped along his spine. Everything that dogs had always stood for—safety, security, guarding hearth and home—had turned topsy-turvy.

He forced himself to read on.

> "When I woke up this morning," Phillips explained, "the back door was open and my dog, Bear, was sound asleep on the entry rug. I thought the wind had blown the door open during the night, but then I discovered that my lures were missing. I had intended to enter the Great Lure competition this weekend. The whole situation is growing quite worrisome!"

Seagulls screeched and circled above the grocery store. The scent of meat scraps hit

Kito's nose. He bolted from the newspaper stand to the back of the grocery store.

"Last piece," Mr. Erickson called. "Here, Kito," he said, tossing the treat in his direction. "You almost missed out."

Kito caught the meat scrap in midair as a seagull swooped overhead, complaining. Smacking his lips, he glanced up. From the upstairs apartment, Tundra looked down at him through one of the windows.

Kito whined, then groaned, then worked himself up into a full-scale round of barking. Pretty soon Chester and Gunnar caught on and joined in.

Mr. Erickson shifted his gaze from the dogs to the upstairs window. "Oh, I get it. You want her to come out and play? I suppose I could climb the stairs and coax her outside. Heck, it'll do her good."

Moments later the back door opened and Mr. Erickson nudged Tundra outside.

She shrugged her big white shoulders. "Hi," she said sheepishly. "Looks like I'm forced outside. Not that I want to be here.

What do I have to live for these days?"

The other three dogs pressed closer.

"Live for?" Chester said. "Criminy rawhide chews, Tundra! We need you, how about that?"

Kito met her eyes. "Three burglaries in three days, that's why."

"Three?" she said. "You're telling me that mine wasn't the only place robbed?"

"That's right," Kito replied.

"How dooooo yooooou knooooow?"

Kito had to think fast. He vowed to keep his reading secret to himself. "I overheard some talk from villagers," he fudged. "Apparently it's in this morning's paper."

Tundra sat taller, towering over them. "I'm not saying I'll come back as your leader," she said. "But I'll help if I can. Fill me in on things before we get to the fire hydrant."

Kito filled her in on their failed efforts to bait the burglar by planting the stolen fishing lure. He told her about catching a glimpse of someone—or something—fleeing the Tweet residence. He told her that Bear had apparently been home when Angelica Phillips's home was robbed.

"Bear?" Tundra repeated. "Someone got past him, too? We'd better go and see if anyone knows more."

At that, they took off. Dogs were gathered at the fire hydrant as they neared. Chocolate and Snowball were chattering away, encircled by the other dogs.

"No, no, no," Chocolate said in a rush. "We were definitely not home when our house was robbed."

"That's right," Snowball joined in. "Otherwise we wouldn't have let anyone past us! We might be young, but we could be tough if we had to be." *Yip-yip-yip!* She let out a high-pitched bark to prove her point.

Bear, Schmitty, Lucky, Muffin, and Willow listened in, but they shifted their attention at the sight of Tundra approaching. They lowered themselves closer to the ground out of respect.

"Y'all! Sweet sassafras! Tundra's back!"

Muffin cried, jumping up and down and spinning in circles, then flattening her body to the sidewalk. "Your Majesty!"

Tundra sat curbside, keeping her distance. "I'm here to help, that's all. I'm barely fit to be a member of Dog Watch, let alone your alpha dog."

The dogs started to protest, but she showed her teeth and growled them into silence.

"Well, then," Kito started, clearing his throat, "let's have a meeting." He brought the other dogs up to speed, then asked for any new findings.

"Bear," he said, "I understand your home was burglarized too."

Bear hung his head. With his bulky size and thick, black hair, tourists often mistook him for a real bear at first glance. He looked fierce, but inside, Kito knew Bear to be as gentle as a teddy bear. "All I'm saying is . . . I didn't stop the burglar."

"Did you hear someone enter?" asked Lucky.

"Yup." Bear wouldn't meet their eyes.

"Did you see them?" Schmitty asked.

"Nope." He lowered his head, acting just as Tundra had after the first burglary.

"Did you smell them?" Chester asked.

"Nope." His voice faded to barely a whisper.

"Chompin' chicken livers!" cried Chester, his tail straight up. "If you couldn't see the burglar or smell the burglar, then what do we possibly have to go on? What are we up against here, anyway?"

An uneasy silence wove among them.

"Maybe an *alien*," said Schmitty, glancing around nervously.

"Oooh—from outer space?" Willow exclaimed. "That's scary! Gives me dog bumps! I mean, what if they want to take dogs back to their planet for research?"

"Well, I suppose anything's possible," Kito said respectfully.

Chester rolled his eyes.

"I'm so sorry," Bear said. "I was worthless." Then he ambled off toward home.

Kito didn't know what to think. He waited,

hoping Tundra would take charge now that she'd joined them, if at a distance. But she wouldn't say a word. Someone had to get things pointed in the right direction.

"Dog Watch," he said, circling the dogs, weaving in and out among them, "needs every dog's skills if we're going to solve this threat. Our people are frightened. We dogs are discouraged. These are not signs of a healthy and safe village." He quoted a line he'd read once from a book about presidents. "'The only thing we have to fear,'" he said, "'is fear itself.'"

He needed to believe those words, the words of Franklin Delano Roosevelt. He let the words sink in, let them touch the heart of each and every dog. Inside, Kito trembled, but he forced himself to act brave.

"Now is the time for courage," he said. "Now is the time for all good dogs to unite. Now is the time for Dog Watch to get to work. Now is the time for an action plan."

"Y'all, fishin' opens tomorrow mornin'," said Muffin. She placed her front feet on the hydrant. "And that competition is tomorrow evenin'. Way I see this, we better be aimin' to catch that burglar before then. Otherwise, I suspect they'll be fixin' to leave town right after the competition."

"That's right, Muffin," said Lucky. "This burglar seems intent on taking lures. Could be they're interested in entering the best ones in the competition, or it could be they found this patch the best berry picking, so to speak."

Schmitty's back hairs bristled. "Set me on this burglar. I'll solve this problem in no time."

Sitting curbside, Tundra spoke up. "There's something you haven't told me yet, Kito and Chester."

Kito felt a familiar flush of guilt rush through him. He'd told her about stealing the Hollinghorsts' fishing lure. Did she suspect he could read?

"You're both sporting green paws. There must be an explanation, right?"

Chester lowered his head. "It was my doing. In my excitement over Kito's brilliant idea to bait the burglar, I knocked over a paint can with my tail."

Kito glanced at his green feet. It was embarrassing, hardly the look of a dignified dog. "Unfortunately," he said, "my *brilliant* plan failed miserably."

Tundra closed her eyes briefly, the way she did when she was on the verge of an idea. When she opened them again, a familiar spark of intelligence flashed in her eyes. "If that green paint stuck to your paws, why couldn't paint stick to the shoes of a burglar? If we put our minds to it, we just might catch our burglar like a fly in syrup."

"Beefy nuggets, that's excellent!" Chester said.

Tundra raised herself up taller as the purple truck roared past.

"A flyyyyyy can't flyyyyyy out of syrup," said Gunnar, "but couldn't our buuuurglar walk ouuuut of paaaaint?"

"My hope exactly," said Tundra. "Walk out and leave tracks behind. A paint path—for Dog Watch to follow!"

**10**

# The Action Plan

**Midmorning, when Kito** and Chester headed home, Mrs. Hollinghorst stood by the station wagon. She lifted the hatch. "Vet appointments, boys. Hop in!"

"Good greasy gravy!" Chester jumped up. "A dog's life is never his own!"

"Just be glad you get to roam as much as you do," Kito reminded him. "How would you like to be kenneled all day, every day, like some poor dogs?"

In the examination room, the veterinarian's braids touched her white doctor's coat. She hoisted Kito onto the stainless steel table. His paws slipped and he shivered with dread, but he tried to stay calm. The sooner they finished, the sooner they could get back to their action plan.

"Kito, other than your green paws," she said with a chuckle, "you look healthy as can be." With one hand she offered him a delicious, chunky treat and with the other she stuck a needle into the loose skin of his neck. He felt the prick, but before he knew it, he was gobbling a *second* treat and barely noticed the second shot at all. "That's it," she said, lifting him off the table. "Next!"

Under the nearby desk, Chester cowered. Mrs. Hollinghorst kneeled beside him, trying to coax him out. "Oh, it's not that bad, Chester. You've been here before. You know Dr. Molly won't hurt you!"

"I hate shots," Chester said to Kito, who sat down beside the door.

"Hey, buddy, the sooner you get it over with, the sooner we get back home."

"Here, allow me," the vet said. She reached down, treat in hand, and scooped Chester in her arms. He whimpered, whined, wailed, and carried on as if he was going to be fitted with a dog muzzle.

"Oh, Chester, I'm not going to hurt you." She reached in her pocket and kept an endless supply of treats coming, which Chester focused on intently. One by one by one by one . . . "Yum, yum."

Within minutes the vet announced, "All done! What a good dog!"

On the exam table, Chester twisted his head back and forth, looking for more treats. "Wait, she hasn't given me my shot yet. I should get more treats."

Kito glanced up at the table. "You goofy beagle. You were so busy munching, you didn't even notice. She gave you *two* shots!"

"Beggin' biscuits!" he said, licking his lips.

When they reached home, the shots made the dogs drowsy. They curled up in the entryway on the braided rug and slept away the whole afternoon.

• • •

The smoky, grease-sizzling smell of hamburgers on the grill rousted them from their snooze. They jumped up, ready for action. "Remember," Kito said. "We stick close by our owners, right until bedtime. When the opportunity is right, we have to be ready to put our action plan into effect."

"Roger that," Chester replied. "In the meantime, we have some serious begging to do. A dog's gotta be a dog, too, not just a crime stopper."

"I'm with you there, Chester." Kito lifted his nose to the air and scratched to be let outside.

Mrs. H opened the door and stepped out with the dogs to join Mr. H at the grill. The burgers sizzled and spat and sent up a lovely odor. The dogs sat, tails wrapped around their haunches, noses focused on the grill.

"Honey," Mrs. H said, "if these burglaries are about fishing lures, then I don't want our home to be robbed next!"

"You think our dogs are going to let somebody into our place without putting up a big fuss?" He flipped a burger. "My concern is where I misplaced my Trouble-Jig. But getting robbed? We don't have to worry."

"But honey, that's probably what Mr. Erickson thought. And I bet Angelica Phillips felt the same way. Tundra and Bear are the village's biggest dogs. I mean, something doesn't add up. The thief must be someone the Pembrook dogs know very well."

"Like who?"

"I don't know for sure, but maybe someone they see every single day. Someone they trust! Someone like the newspaper carrier or—"

"Howie? Oh, he wouldn't steal. But you might be onto something."

Kito and Chester exchanged glances.

"She makes a good point," Kito said.

Mrs. H stepped into the house and returned with two glasses of water with lemon wedges.

"Well, if not Howie . . . ," said Mr. H, salting and peppering the burgers. Kito's mouth watered, despite his best efforts to keep his mind on the conversation. "Mr. Cutler?"

Mrs. H sat down in a wood-slatted chair. "I really don't think so. Ever since he apologized for the parade disaster and painted the fire hydrant like Raggedy Ann, he's been nothing but sweet. What about Mavis, the postmaster? The dogs see her all the time. Or Mr. Erickson at the grocery store? He feeds the dogs scraps every day. All the dogs know him."

"Mavis? Mr. Erickson? They would never steal. And why would Mr. Erickson report a burglary if he was the burglar?"

"I know it doesn't seem logical, honey. I'm just trying to think outside the box."

When the conversation turned to Mr. H's next book, Kito and Chester took up where their owners had left off.

Chester sat squarely in front of Kito. "I know who our thief is."

"You do? Well, tell me."

"Our very own mayor."

"Mr. Jorgenson? You've got to be kidding, Chester. He wouldn't stoop so low as to steal from his fellow villagers. It can't be him."

"Beefy biscuits, Kito! If you're going to be a good detective, you have to think outside the box, just like Mrs. H said. Just answer me this: Who was the first over here to warn the Hollinghorsts about their collection?"

"The mayor."

"Righto. Who knows enough about lures in our village to judge them at the competition?"

"Our mayor."

"Bingo! And who was there on the scene just seconds after the Tweets came home to their burglarized house?"

"Okay, okay. The mayor. I get your point, but that doesn't mean—"

Chester sniffed the air, following the curling smoke from the grill until he nearly fell off the side of the deck. "Oops. Where was I?"

"He has a degree in psychology, Chester. We should be calling him Dr. Jorgenson, only 'Doctor' and 'Mayor' aren't usually used at the same time in a person's title. But he knows people and he—"

"Bloody right he does. He's just the sort of chum who would understand *when* and *where* to strike. He knows this village inside and out!"

Kito lay down. Burgers grilling or not, this was making his snout ache. He really, really liked Mr. Jorgenson. He always led the village parades with enthusiasm, and he tried to use empathy at the council meetings—though when that didn't work, he was forced to use his yellow megaphone. The mayor stealing lures? If this was true, then something was truly rotten in Pembrook.

Just then the door of the neighboring house opened. Mr. Jorgenson waved and swaggered over. "Sure smells good," he said in an extra-cheerful tone. "I just learned that a big film crew from Duluth is coming up to film the competition. The Big Fish, Great Lure contest is going to put Pembrook on the map!"

Kito's lip curled, and he let out a low, barely audible growl. Chester's back hairs formed a ridge sharp as a dorsal fin.

"What's up with your dogs?" Mr. Jorgenson asked. He took three steps back toward his own yard. "They sure are edgy today. A case of mistaken paranoia, perhaps? Projecting their fears onto others?"

"Oh, the boys got their shots today," Mrs. H explained. "They might be feeling a little out of sorts. Please don't take it personally."

"Maybe I'll visit later," the mayor said, "when they're feeling, um, better." He headed back to his house. The dogs watched the mayor's every move. At his doorstep, the mayor glanced back uneasily at the dogs, then disappeared inside.

"I can't wait until sunset," Kito said, "to set the trap."

"We'll catch him red-handed," Chester added, "or at least paint-pawed!"

# 11

# Paint Trap

**That evening Kito** and Chester hovered in the garage as Mr. and Mrs. H put the finishing touches on their last lures. The dogs paced back and forth by the workshop bench.

Beyond the open garage door, the Tweet girls were riding their bikes up and down the street, with Chocolate and Snowball racing behind them. Spring peepers sang out from a nearby pond, filling the air with their squeaky frog song.

"The rest of the dogs are counting on us," Kito said. In a majority vote, Dog Watch had agreed that the best plan was to catch the burglar by leaving the Hollinghorst lure collection available for stealing. That way, along with a little paint, they'd be sure to catch their thief. Kito still worried about the plan. What if they lost the whole collection of lures to this thief? Though the other dogs had assured him that this time they would catch the burglar and get all the lures back, even the Trouble-Jig, Kito couldn't rest until then. His belly was wobbly with worry.

He sat back and scratched under his collar with his hind foot, which helped ease his worries, at least some. "We've managed to solve the first step in our action plan, but let's review for practice."

"Righto! Now you're thinking like a British detective," Chester replied, planting himself right next to Kito.

"Okay, the moment Mrs. H hangs up her painting smock, you use your beagle snout to nudge a can of paint under the table before she has time to put a lid on it and notice it gone."

"Ten-four, good buddy."

Kito settled into scratching the back of his ears. "Then, when the time is right, you'll spill it—this time on purpose—right in front of the workshop table."

"Roger that! Right in front of the table of lures! Just what we need to catch our lure-snatching burglar! He'll step in the paint and we'll track him down. 'Course, that won't be so hard, since he lives right next door."

"We can't make assumptions," Kito said.

"Buttery biscuits, who else? Every dog in the village trusts the mayor. That explains his getting past Bear and Tundra. Plus, he's the expert on lures!"

"Let's get back to the plan. We need to review. The only piece we haven't put together yet is the garage door. Somehow we need to make sure it stays open. We know Mr. and Mrs. H will air out the garage until they go to bed, but we have to see that the door stays open *all* night. But how are we going to do that?" He paced, glancing at the garage-door button on the wall. "Wait," he said. "I've got it! The moment Mr. or Mrs. H pushes the garage door button, I'll scratch on the entry door to go out. If I time it right, they'll step in from the garage and let me outside. I'll have just about six seconds to dash back in under the garage door before it closes completely!"

"Under the garage door? Good gizzards, Kito! There's no need to sacrifice your life! Not over fishing lures, no matter how valuable! Mr. and Mrs. H would feel worse about losing you than one of their lures."

Kito had to smile to himself. "Chester, what would I do without you? You're such a friend, through thick and thin. Don't worry. I'm not going to get killed. Haven't you seen what happens if you step under our new garage door as it's coming down?"

"No. Why would I want to do that?" Chester looked disgusted. "Beagles come from a higher stock of hound than that. I'm sure my British relatives and ancestors would never think of playing such a dangerous game with a garage door and—"

"Chester. Stop. The door doesn't squash

you, it goes right back up the second anything crosses the infrared safety light. While I'm doing that, you create a distraction somewhere so that our owners won't hear that the garage door didn't close."

Mrs. H's voice came from behind them. "That should do it, honey," she said, setting the last lure down on the workshop table. "Should be dry by morning. Let's get to bed. We'll be up awfully early fishing and it will be a long day with the competition tomorrow." She took off her smock and hung it on a peg, and then she gave Mr. H a quick smooch.

At that, the dogs whipped themselves into action. They raced and zipped around the garage, as if playing chase. But before the Hollinghorsts realized what was going on, the red wheelbarrow tilted and crashed on its side. A ladder slid down a wall, its legs knocked out from under it. Kito ran around and around their legs as Chester went to work on hiding a small, open can of paint.

"What's gotten into you two?" Mrs. H put

her hands on her hips and glared at Kito. "There's no chipmunk in here! Now settle down before you knock something over again. That green paint was hard enough to clean up!"

"Maybe they need a walk to burn off some extra energy," said Mr. H.

"Oh, honey. We have to get up so early. Let's just get them settled down for the night, okay? Now where's Chester?"

Chester emerged from beneath the workshop table. "You are certainly a goofy pair of dogs," said Mr. H. "Let's head in."

Mrs. H stepped into the house first, and Mr. H held the door for the dogs. Chester lingered behind, but quickly caught up as Mr. H pressed the garage door button. "Time to close things up."

The garage door rumbled and began its slow slide down the metal runners. "Go, go, go!" Chester said, talking faster than the auctioneers who occasionally passed through Pembrook. "Make a fuss to be let out the entry door!"

"But the paint—did you—"

"It's waiting for you. A pretty shade of purple!"

At that, Kito scratched furiously and whined at the front door. "For the love of peanut butter," Mr. H said with a frustrated sigh. "Okay, Kito!"

The entry door opened slightly. Kito flew out just as the garage door was nearing the ground. He raced for the long, wide garage door, intending to cross through the invisible infrared light that stretched from one edge of the door to the other. The garage door rattled and rumbled, coming closer and closer to his back. What if Chester was right? What if the door squashed him? He really didn't want to lose his life!

From inside the house, only confirming his gut fears, a mournful song rose to a terrible crescendo. Chester was singing a sorrowful tune at the top of his beagle lungs. A sad, desperate beagle song.

# 12

# Footprints

**Kito was sure** he would be squashed. But then, in that small suspended second in time when death hovered over him, he stepped through the right spot—and the garage door reversed and went back up again.

He had survived! The plan had worked! The garage was now wide open for any burglar to see.

With a quick glance around, he made sure Mr. H hadn't stepped from the house or back into the garage. The coast was clear. Chester's wailing had done the trick and kept Mr. and Mrs. H from hearing the garage door change its course.

Before he lost the opportunity, Kito darted back in. He needed to be fast, but not reckless. One bump into a wheelbarrow or lawn mower could send the Hollinghorsts running to investigate. Carefully he crept to the workbench and peered into the shadows under it. A half-full can of purple paint rested in the corner. Kito grabbed the handle in his teeth, lifted it toward him, then set it down on the cement floor beneath the workbench. Using his snout, he nudged the can onto its edge and tipped it sideways until it dropped over, spreading purple paint into a puddle. Careful not to step into the paint, Kito eased off to the side and stood back to examine his handiwork.

With darkness coming on, a burglar would never see the paint on the floor. Maybe someone would use a flashlight to examine the table's contents, but it wasn't likely they'd shine the light below the workbench table. Kito's tail curved proudly over his back.

This time they couldn't lose.

Satisfied, he turned away, stepped out of the garage, and sat at the entry door, alternately whining and barking.

On cue, just as he had hoped, Mrs. H opened the door. "Come on in, Kito," she said kindly. "Let's head upstairs. Time for some shut-eye."

Chester met him. "Well? Did you find the purple paint? Did you spill it by the table? Is the garage door open?"

"Affirmative on all counts," Kito said, heading up the spiral staircase. "All systems go. All we need now is our burglar."

Kito and Chester slept so soundly they didn't hear the Hollinghorsts get up the next morning. Voices climbed the stairs to the master bedroom.

"I always close the garage door," said Mr. H, "and I'm sure I closed it last night, too."

Kito bolted upright in his dog bed. Chester jumped from the Hollinghorsts' bed. They nearly tumbled down the stairs together.

"Think it worked?" Chester asked.

"Let's hope."

They slipped through the open door leading to the garage. The Hollinghorsts stood back from the workshop table, which was completely cleared of fishing lures.

"Our burglar took the bait!" Chester exclaimed. "Snooping sausages! All the lures! This is perfect!"

"That part's good, but look at our owners. This makes my stomach turn."

Mr. and Mrs. H leaned into one another, staring at the empty table. "Who would do this?" Mr. H moaned. "Who would steal all our lures? It was bad enough that my Trouble-Jig disappeared. I hoped I'd misplaced it. But this proves that it was no accident. Someone came in earlier, cased out our place, and decided to come back."

Mrs. H's shoulders drooped, and she let out a long sigh.

"Check out the footprints!" Chester said, sniffing the dried purple shoe prints on the cement floor. "Ha! These tracks will lead us right to him. With my nose and your eyes,

Kito, they don't stand a chance now." He sniffed the floor around the Hollinghorsts' slippered feet.

Mrs. H turned from the empty workshop table, squatted beside Chester, and put her arms around his body. "Oh, Chester. You're upset too! Why—" She glanced around the floor. "I didn't notice these prints. Honey, look!"

Mr. H scanned the garage floor. "Well I'll be. If someone hadn't left their footprints behind, I would have blamed our dogs for spilling another can of paint."

Putting her forefinger across her lips, Mrs. H studied the paint. "At least the green and purple complement each other. Makes a rather interesting pattern . . . almost impressionistic, don't you think?"

"Good gravy and milk bones," Chester said, following the paint prints toward the open garage door.

"Okay, Chester," Mr. H said. "You probably smell something strange. You know someone was here last night, don't you, boy?"

Chester wagged his tail wildly.

"And we'd better get fishing," said Mrs. H. "It's just too bad we can't use our homemade lures."

The dogs stepped beyond the garage door, noses to the dried prints. An icy wind cuffed them sideways, but they barely noticed.

At the edge of the road, the purple prints ended abruptly at a pair of plain brown leather shoes.

"Shoes? Where did the prints go?" Kito looked left toward the community building, across the street toward the Tweets' church-home, and to the right where the mayor lived. "What good are a pair of brown leather shoes?"

"Buddy," Chester said, sniffing the shoes, "for once, I'm way ahead of you. Our burglar got away in a vehicle and decided to leave his shoes behind."

Kito stepped closer.

The shoes were flipped sideways and purple paint covered each sole. "It's our burglar's shoes, all right." He examined them closer. On the inside of one shoe, he noticed the words "Hush Puppies." He had no idea what that meant. Was it a code? Were they supposed to be quiet about the shoes? Then he noticed something else that faded out: "Siz . . ." He didn't know what that meant either. Then he had an idea. "Hey, Chester, all we have to do is match these shoes to their owner," he said, glancing over his shoulder.

Inside the garage, the Hollinghorsts stood side by side, arms crossed, looking out in bewilderment toward the road. "A pair of shoes! How strange."

Chester picked up a shoe in his teeth.

"Chester, no!" called Mr. H. "Those aren't yours. Put that down."

"We need one for evidence," Kito said. "Let's take off. Pretend you're just playing a game with it."

Together they tore down Pine Street, bumping into each other as they went, not really sure where they were heading. They veered right from Pine Street to Main and kept running. When they couldn't hear Mr. H calling any longer, and they were well out of view, they stopped at the park.

Panting, Chester dropped the shoe in the grass. Kito looked around. No children were out playing on the swings and slides, but that wasn't surprising. The weather was truly foul. The wind whipped up pellets of ice, flinging them right into the dogs' eyes.

"Terrible weather for the Fishing Opener!" Chester pushed his snout in the shoe and rooted and snuffled. "Mmmmm. Stinky."

"Oh, bad weather won't stop people who love to fish," Kito answered. "And it won't stop Dog Watch, either." Kito scanned the park's boundaries for suspicious vehicles or passersby.

"If Mayor Jorgenson is our wrongdoer," Chester said, snuffling deeper in the shoe, "not that I know what his feet smell like, but if it's him, then he must have walked barefoot to his house with the stash of stolen lures."

"*If* he walked," Kito said. "I'm thinking drove."

"But the mayor doesn't drive, remember? It's his mom who always drives 'Baby' the truck around Pembrook."

"Exactly."

"Someone who drives. Could be that food delivery guy."

"Maybe, but to get past Tundra and Bear, remember, it would have to be someone they were really comfortable with. Someone they knew. Not a stranger."

Chester started to chew on the edge of the shoe.

"Hey, cut that out. We need that for evidence. You can't chew it to pieces."

"But what good is it?" Chester asked, flopping down beside the shoe with his snout between his outstretched paws. "Are we going to every house in Pembrook with this shoe and bark and see if whoever steps out has the same size foot?"

"That would take forever," Kito said. "And half the village will be out fishing pretty soon. I say we bring the shoe to the hydrant. Let every dog examine it—the size, the shape, the smell. We're certain to get a positive identification on it."

"Brilliant, Kito! I knew you'd come up with a plan!" he shouted, jumping to his feet again. "Morning or night, Pembrook dogs unite!"

Kito joined in the chorus, then sat back, lifted his head higher yet, and barked out the announcement:

"Emergency meeting! Emergency meeting! All dogs to the hydrant! All dogs to the hydrant!"

# 13

# Reeling in a Big Fish

**Leather shoe in** mouth, Chester took off for the fire hydrant. Kito raced alongside him as dogs throughout the village took up the chorus: "Morning or night, Pembrook dogs unite! Morning or night, Pembrook dogs unite!"

As fast as cats being chased, dogs of every size, shape, and age gathered at the fire hydrant.

Mavis, the postmaster, was hoisting the flag up the flagpole. "What's the big meeting?" she asked. "All your owners out fishing already? I s'pose today's the big day."

Then she headed inside the post office and put the OPEN sign on the door.

Wind shoved dark and heavy rainclouds across the sky. Kito glanced around. With Tundra sitting at a distance beside the curb again, he felt forced to take charge. He sat next to the hydrant and scanned the pack of dogs as they circled around him.

"Well, we're going to find the burglar who has been causing so much trouble in our village and bring him to justice!"

The dogs murmured their agreement.

"So take a good look at this shoe," Kito ordered, as Chester walked from dog to dog with the shoe hanging from his mouth. "The action plan we discussed yesterday went off as smoothly as greyhounds round a racetrack. A short time ago, we found this shoe, and it belongs to the very man—"

"Or woman," Lucky chimed in. "You can't make assumptions."

"Lucky, in general, that's true," Kito said. "But study this shoe closely."

Chester dropped the shoe in front of

Lucky, who sniffed it inside and out.

"Does this look like a shoe you've seen any woman in our village wear? Do you know of any woman with a foot that big?"

"Well, none that I've ever seen in Pembrook."

"I rest my case. We're dealing with a man. Now, looking at and sniffing this shoe, who can tell me who it belongs to? Soon as we identify this shoe's owner, we can speedily bring him to justice. Anyone?" Kito scanned the dogs' serious faces. Even Schmitty frowned at the shoe.

"Anyone have a guess, at least?"

The dogs took turns examining the shoe, but every dog was silent. This wasn't what he had hoped for. How could they be dead-ended so quickly?

Tundra spoke up from her distant post. "Let's keep a lookout for anyone who matches the scent of those shoes. If every dog fans out, we'll cover the farthest reaches of the village. By the time the fishing boats return and the competition is underway this afternoon, we'll certainly have some good leads—if not our thief."

"Roger that plan!" Chester said.

Then the dogs dispersed, meandering every which way. Schmitty joined Chester and Kito, sniffing the road and parked vehicles with empty boat trailers. They closed in on the docks just beyond the grocery store and Woody's Fairly Reliable Guide Service. Whitecaps raked the big bay and tossed fishing boats around like rubber dog toys. The dogs trotted to the edge of the longest pier.

"This is not weather for beast or man," Chester said, "or AKC-registered beagles, either."

"Hey," Kito said, scanning the bay. Two people in yellow rain suits were busy reeling in and netting a big, flopping fish. "Isn't that Mr. and Mrs. H out there?"

Chester squinted. "Looks like that tennis couple to me. Let's hope our owners have better luck luring in fish than we're having with our burglar."

"That's for sure," Kito replied. "They certainly can't win anything in the Great Lure part of the contest."

"So the burglar took all their lures?" Schmitty asked.

"Every single one," Kito replied. "Mr. and Mrs. H are probably fishing with worms."

"Wiggly worms!" Chester groaned. "Hot dog chunks would be better!"

The day passed slowly. No significant leads. No significant matches of smells to the shoe that Chester carried around all day. And the longer he carried it, the more his teeth marks formed permanent grooves, and the more teeth marks on the shoe, the harder it was for Chester to resist chewing it.

By late in the afternoon, the Hollinghorsts returned and tied their boat up to their dock with a stringer of three big fish. This time Chester and Kito were on the dock to meet them. Chester dropped the shoe and peered over the edge of the dock to watch the fish swimming on the stringer. "Look at that big one! They might have a winner!"

Kito stared at the leather shoe. It was well chewed and soft with dog spit. He was disgusted at Chester's lack of self-control. "This shoe looks like a leather chew."

"No wonder you two wouldn't come when we called you," said Mrs. H, the rain splattering the top of her hood. "Guess you thought you'd found a treat on the road, huh?" She picked up the shoe in one hand and a lunchbox in the other and headed toward the house. "We're off to the community building. We have half a chance at the Big Fish contest."

"Sure wish we had our lures," Mr. H added, following behind.

When the Hollinghorsts put their biggest fish in a cooler and carried it to the community building, Kito and Chester trotted after them. The temperature dropped, and though it was mid-May, rain turned to sleet. Kito hoped they'd be able to go inside and get out of the nasty weather.

Mayor Jorgenson greeted villagers at the door with a big smile on his round face. Kito and Chester sneaked past him.

"See that smile?" Chester said.

"Yeah."

"It's because he's going to win the contest."

"Judges can't enter contests."

"Yeah, but he's the mayor and the judge. Why can't he make the rules? I bet you anything he enters stolen lures and wins!"

The community building was swimming with fish in coolers and villagers and dogs. Everyone had a fish story to tell, and some— Angelica Phillips, the Tweets, Mr. Erickson, the Hollinghorsts, and a few others—talked about having their homes and garages broken into and their lures stolen.

"I hope whoever did it gets caught," said Mrs. H. "I'll sleep better when that happens."

"I agree!" said Angelica Phillips, as she lifted her camera from around her neck and started taking pictures of the Great Lures table. But a mere six lures were displayed on the white tablecloth. Bear hovered meekly beside her, not saying a word.

"The judging will begin in five minutes!"

called Mayor Jorgenson through his yellow megaphone. "The winner of the greatest lure will receive one week of free dinners at the local café. The winner with the biggest fish will receive two hundred fifty dollars in cash. Who knows, maybe some lucky person will win both!"

The crowd of villagers talked among themselves.

Kito turned to Chester. "Something's wrong. The burglar *isn't* here."

"What do you mean? Every person from the village is here today. He's gotta be here."

"No, I can feel it. He's not here. It's way too calm for me. If something was wrong, I'd feel it under my skin." He paced uneasily around the room, then veered toward the windows, with Chester at his heels.

Kito stared out. The purple truck was parked outside the community building with its matching boat already loaded on its trailer. Where were its owners? Then he spotted them. A round-bellied, white-haired couple held hands as they approached the community building steps. When they entered, Kito and Chester scurried toward them, staying out of arm's reach.

"They're strangers," Kito said, "but my insides are as calm as a glassy lake."

"Four minutes until judging!" Mayor Jorgenson announced.

"Once the competition is over," Chester said, "I'm sure our burglar will be long gone too."

Kito trotted back to the windows again, with Chester muttering behind him. A familiar red and white truck, its windshield wipers flapping, drove past the post office and tavern. As it passed the community building, Kito spotted its driver. At the wheel, Jeremy Jones—with his lean face and hunched, narrow shoulders—looked out at them and tipped his hat toward the building and the dogs.

He should have known it! He'd had his eyes so set on finding a burglar who knew every dog, but his thinking had led him astray.

That was their man! He couldn't prove it, but his instincts shouted at him. The Schwankl Frozen Foods delivery truck slowed down slightly, then started to increase its speed.

Kito's fur stood straight as matchsticks. A growl formed in his belly and rumbled in his throat. There were times when instincts were more useful than brains! He started barking out commands as he ran to the door. "Every dog! At attention! Follow me!"

Six dogs bolted as one from the community building and into the storm.

"Stop him!" Kito shouted. "But don't get under the truck wheels!"

Sleet had changed to hail and slicked sidewalks and the road beneath their paws with sheer ice. The dogs put up a fearsome racket, baying and barking as they raced beside the Schwankl truck. With a chorus of barking, they called in every dog from the village. Dogs raced after the truck and snapped at its wheels.

Clawing for traction on the icy road, the dogs slipped and slid, tumbled and rolled, but found their footing and exploded in mighty bursts behind the truck. Tongues hung out sideways, flopping in the wind.

"Faster!" Schmitty called. "Don't let him get away!"

Gunnar bellowed as he ran, "Slooooooow down!"

With every ounce of energy, the dogs barked and yipped and tried to outrace the truck.

The truck passed Pembrook Park, swerved back and forth to avoid the dogs, but stayed on the road and shifted into a higher, faster gear. Its giant black tires splashed through icy puddles, covering the dogs with gravel and mud. Kito took a faceful, blinking back water and grit. His throat and chest burned from running and barking, but he kept on after the truck.

"Cheesy dog bones!" Chester called. "Don't let him get away!"

But to Kito's dismay, the truck shifted gears again and picked up speed, increasing the distance between them as it neared the outskirts of Pembrook.

# Meatball Madness

**Just as the** red and white truck sped up and approached the village limits, it switched into an even higher gear. A speed they couldn't match. Kito's heart sank. Their thief was going to get away! Jeremy Jones in his Schwankl Frozen Foods truck had only one corner to round before reaching the two-lane highway beyond. Once he reached that, they'd never catch up with him.

Just as the truck rounded the corner to the highway, Jeremy Jones waved at the dogs in his side mirrors.

In the same instant the speeding vehicle

slid on the icy road, and despite the sound of screeching brakes, it swerved left—then right—then left! The truck careened off the icy road and into the rain-filled ditch, tipping slightly as it slid. The truck's rear door bumped open and mounds of frozen foods spilled out.

The dogs raced to the truck as Jeremy Jones climbed out in stocking feet. He held up his hands like a true thief caught in the act of doing something wrong. "Hold on, dogs. You don't need to get your ruffs up." With his hands still up, he walked to the back of his truck.

Kito growled. He showed his teeth, but the calm manner of Jeremy Jones confused him for a moment. Had he gotten things all wrong?

Then the deliveryman held up a few bags of frozen meatballs. He ripped them open and flung their contents across the wet grass. "Here you go! This should keep you distracted!"

At that, Tundra leaped closer to the man. She held her white German shepherd body rigid, and she stood as tall as Kito had ever seen her. She was menacing, frightening in her stance. She called out to the other dogs.

"Stop!" she growled. "I forbid Pembrook dogs from so much as *sniffing* one of those meatballs!"

Chester whined and took a step back from the meatball between his front paws.

"Oh, just one bite," Schmitty complained.

"I mean it! Kito, go get the villagers down here. I don't care how you do it, but do it."

"Yes, ma'am!" He took off for the community building at top speed, slipping on ice as he went. Outside the door, he heard Mayor Jorgenson's megaphone. "Ready to begin the Great Lure and Big Fish judging!"

Kito pawed at the windows and barked and whined until every villager looked out his way. When Mr. and Mrs. H stepped out, Kito tried to lead them down the street toward the highway. Finally, they must have looked far enough to see the pack of dogs and the truck in the ditch.

"Wait up!" called Mrs. H. "We all better go help the truck in the ditch!"

At that, the mayor postponed the competition and villagers donned raincoats and slickers and headed out after Kito. What they found was Jeremy Jones, braced up against the delivery truck's back door. Village dogs pinned him there, refusing to back down.

"Sorry about our dogs," said the mayor. "Looks like your back door is busted pretty good."

"Oh, it'll be fine," said Jeremy Jones, sweat pouring from his forehead despite the frigid air. "Just need a little push here to get my truck back on the road." He pushed against the door as if to demonstrate, but all of a sudden, the bent door fell off its hinges completely.

Out spilled more frozen pies, pizzas, vegetables, meatballs—and lure after painted wooden fishing lure!

"Well, well, well," said Mayor Jorgenson. "Isn't this interesting! Looks like our dogs caught the biggest fish of the day!"

Kito and Chester exchanged glances. Mayor Jorgenson got on his cell phone. In minutes a county sheriff vehicle pulled up with its lights flashing, and Jeremy Jones was escorted away in handcuffs to the county jail.

As the villagers dispersed and a tow truck came to haul away the frozen foods truck, the dogs clustered together.

"Bear," Tundra said, "I think you and I have a confession to make, don't we?"

"Yup."

"It's humiliating," Tundra began, "but it's time I confess. I was duped by *frozen meatballs*. I let a burglar get past me because of food. He tossed them out to distract me. And eating frozen meatballs temporarily took away my sense of smell—"

"Yup," Bear agreed. "And sense of danger. Before I knew it, someone had come into my home and was gone before I finished the last meatball."

"It's a shameful thing," Tundra said, "and I hope it never happens to any of you. But I've learned my lesson. If you're in trouble, no matter how embarrassing something might be, it's better to speak up and ask for help. Had I put aside my pride and told you that I'd been hoodwinked—well, maybe we could have worked together as a team and caught our burglar sooner."

In unison, the dogs shouted out, "Tundra! Tundra! Tundra!"

Tundra glanced from dog to dog. "Order! Don't forget that rules are rules around here."

Schmitty stepped closer to a meatball. Gunnar nudged one with his nose. "Now can weeeee eeeeeeat?"

Tundra almost smiled. "Most definitely."

The dogs forgot all about the freezing rain and the icy wind. They threw themselves with abandon at the meatballs scattered across the slopes of the ditch. They found meatballs around the truck, under the truck, and in the truck. They rolled in the meatballs. They wrestled over meatballs. They sniffed and chewed and licked and nibbled frozen meatball after frozen meatball.

"A Dog Watch party!" Lucky yelled.

"Woo-whoooooooo!" Gunnar bellowed, stretched on his back, legs up, belly growing rounder with each meatball.

"I love meatballs!" Schmitty added.

"Y'all," Muffin said, dancing in happy circles, "I haven't had this much fun since, well, since I don't know when!"

"Meatball madness," Kito said under his breath as he spotted another meatball under one of the truck's stopped tires. He gobbled it down. He had to admit, bringing in a big fish had never been so much fun!

When the Big Fish, Great Lure competition was finally over, the Hollinghorsts walked home with not just one, not two, but *three* awards. "I can't believe it!" Mrs. H exclaimed. "Because of your grandfather's lure, we won the gift certificate for a week of eating out at the local café. Mr. Erikson is so happy to get his lures back, he's giving every dog a week of doggie treats!"

"Leapin' leftovers!" Chester said, trotting alongside. "An award for our work nailing that crook!"

"Sounds good to me," Kito added.

Ice and sleet covered Pine Street as they slipped and slid toward home. But Kito wasn't worried. Summer, he knew, was just around the corner.

Mr. H reached for Mrs. H's hand. "And two hundred fifty dollars for your winning pike," he said, "is going to help toward your dream."

"Oh? And what's that?"

"More paintbrushes and a *lot* more paint."

She laughed. "Especially more purple and green."

Kito trotted alongside his owners and Chester. He didn't care if their paws were still a silly green. What mattered was that Dog Watch had set things right. Every stolen lure was returned to its rightful owner from the back of the Schwankl Frozen Foods truck. Justice would be served against Jeremy Jones, who had apparently stolen Betty's truck while she was away on vacation. Bear and Tundra had their dignity back. And Dog Watch had their alpha dog back where she belonged—at the top of the pack.

With his tail curved proudly over his back, Kito filled his chest with a breath of crisp, clean air. Once again, all was well in his beloved village of Pembrook.